I ♥ BOOKS

For Roderick

with lots of love from Mum xxx

BLOOMSBURY CHILDREN'S BOOKS
Bloomsbury Publishing Plc
50 Bedford Square, London, WC1B 3DP, UK

BLOOMSBURY, BLOOMSBURY CHILDREN'S BOOKS and the Diana logo
are trademarks of Bloomsbury Publishing Plc

First published in Great Britain 2020 by Bloomsbury Publishing Plc

A catalogue record for this book is available from the British Library

HB: 978 1 4088 9208 4   PB: 978 1 4088 9209 1   eBook: 978 1 4088 9207 7

2 4 6 8 10 9 7 5 3 1

Printed and bound in China by Leo Paper Products, Heshan, Guangdong

All papers used by Bloomsbury Publishing Plc are natural, recyclable products from
wood grown in well managed forests. The manufacturing processes conform to
the environmental regulations of the country of origin

To find out more about our authors and books visit www.bloomsbury.com
and sign up for our newsletters

BEWARE!

Ralfy Rabbit
and the
Secret Book Biter

by Emily MacKenzie

BLOOMSBURY
CHILDREN'S BOOKS
LONDON OXFORD NEW YORK NEW DELHI SYDNEY

Ralfy Rabbit LOVED books.

Small books,

big books,

funny books,

scary books,

adventure
books . . .

and any kind
of other book.

When things were quiet, he
liked nothing more than to
snuggle up with a good book
and **read, read, read.**

The trouble was, things weren't so quiet anymore.

SNIVEL

WAHHHHHH!

SNIFF

SOB

BLUB BOO HOO BLUB BLUB SOB BLUB BLUB

BWAH

Baby Rodney sobbed,
screamed,
shrieked and
snivelled
every time Ralfy
tried to get stuck
into a story.

I ♥

CHARLIE
AND THE
CHOCOLATE
CARROT

GEORGE'S
MARVELLOUS
LETTUCE

STICK
BUN

SHRIEK!

BOO HOO

SNIVEL

SOB

WAILLLLL

WAAAAAA

BOOHOO

BLUB

SOB

And as Rodney got bigger,

the noises he made got bigger, too!

There was just **nowhere** quiet left
for poor Ralfy to read his books.

He tried reading in the
kitchen cupboard.

He tried snuggling in
the linen basket.

He tried hiding in
the garden shed.

Even his favourite bookshop wasn't quiet enough!

There was only **one** thing for it.

Ralfy headed off to the **only place** quiet enough for him to read . . .

The library was Ralfy's favourite place.
He spent hours flicking through the book shelves,
reading stories and deciding which books to borrow.
And best of all – it was quiet!

But when Ralfy got out his book to read, he had a big surprise . . .

There was a **huge hole** in his book.

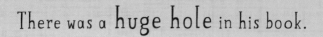

SOMETHING
had taken a bite out of it!

"Did you get a bit **hungry** on the way here, Ralfy?" chuckled the librarian.

"I'm sorry," sniffed Ralfy. "**It wasn't me.**"

"Don't worry," said the librarian. "But maybe you should find out who it was. We need to look after our library books so **everyone** can enjoy them."

Ralfy rushed straight home.

There was a
BOOK BITER
on the loose and
he had to stop them!

Ralfy decided to ask his family first . . .

"I've been too busy **knitting**
to bite books,"
said Granny.

"I've been cooking **carrot crumble**,"
said Dad.

"And I'm **too full** of crumble
to eat books," said Mum.

Clearly it wasn't going to be that easy.

But Ralfy was determined to find out
who the BOOK BITER was.
He picked up his detective kit
and began to investigate.

The bookcase seemed like a good place to look, and as he reached into the shelf, he found something **unexpected**.

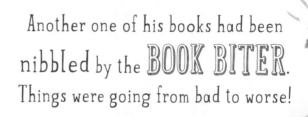

Another one of his books had been **nibbled** by the BOOK BITER. Things were going from bad to worse!

Ralfy reached for another book,
and another and
another...

The covers were tingled
with teeth marks,

chapters had
been **chewed**

and there were
no more happy endings.

All of Ralfy's favourite stories had bits missing from them.

What a MESS!

Suddenly Ralfy heard a noise . . .

It was a snuffling, grunting, rumbling noise.
And it was coming from underneath

THE BUMPER BOOK OF BUNNIES.

The BOOK BITER was **here** and
it was about to be **caught!**

Ralfy crept towards the **noise** . . .

I ♥ BOOKS

It was
Rodney!

THE
BUMPER BOOK
OF
BUNNIES

"Mum!" shouted Ralfy.

"Rodney is the BOOK BITER and
he's eaten ALL my books!"

"Oh, Ralfy! I'm sorry," said Mum.
"Rodney's teeth are growing and
he probably has sore gums.

That sounded painful to Ralfy.
He thought about what he could do to help . . .

LORD
OF
THE
BUNNIES

RALFY'S
MARVELOUS
LETTUCE

STICK
BUN

Ralfy rummaged in
the toy box and handed Rodney
a **rubber rhinoceros** to bite.

He also found a foamy frog
and a squeaky sardine.

But Rodney just
started to cry.

Ralfy thought about what had made him happy
when he was little like Rodney.

And then he had an idea.

He counted out his pocket money and
asked Dad if they could go and
buy Rodney a present.

I ♥ BOOKS

A CLASH of E.A.R.S

CHARLIE AND THE GREAT GLASS LETTUCE

ALICE IN WARREN LAND

HARRY HOPPER and the Deathly meadows

WHERE THE WILD RABBITS ARE

THE GOOD THE BAD, AND THE BUNNY

STICK BUN

HARRY HOPPER and the Half-Blood Fox

FANTASTIC MR BUN

Bunderella

Bu in Boot

I LOVE CARROTS

RABUNZE

RABBITSON CRUSOE

I ♥ BOOKS

So off they went to Ralfy's **other** favourite place...

The bookshop.

Where he found the **ideal** gift for his baby brother.
"I think Rodney will love this one, Dad," said Ralfy.
"Board books are **perfect** for baby bunnies."

Dad smiled. "Ah Ralfy, what a kind big brother you are!
I think **YOU** deserve a present too."

Ralfy gave Rodney his present
as soon as he got home.

"Here you go Rodney – your **very own book!**" said Ralfy.

I ♥ BOOKS

BOOKS

MAKE
GLUE +
BEND

"Why don't you read it to him first?"
suggested Mum.

As he did, the only noise from Rodney
was the sound of him giggling...

and Ralfy realised that perhaps **reading** was something
that he and Rodney could **enjoy together** after all.
(Even if Rodney had a little nibble at the same time!)